Vic stands up to Billy the Bully

"A Book About Courage"

Written by: Latisha Thomas Cokely

Illustrated by: HH-Pax

WestBow Press books may be ordered through booksellers or by contacting:

WestBow Press
A Division of Thomas Nelson & Zondervan
1663 Liberty Drive
Bloomington, IN 47403
www.westbowpress.com
1 (866) 928-1240

ISBN: 978-1-9736-5782-8 (sc)
ISBN: 978-1-9736-5783-5 (e)

Library of Congress Control Number: 2019903516

Print information available on the last page.

WestBow Press rev. date: 8/19/2019

WESTBOW
PRESS®
A DIVISION OF THOMAS NELSON
& ZONDERVAN

Dedication

To Truth & Vic'Tor
You are my greatest inspirations!
(We love because HE first loved us)

To Mom & Dad
Thank you for my amazing childhood and the blessing of the *Power of Positive Thinking*!

In memory of Kevin T. Thomas
The most amazing dream-chaser I've ever known – thank you for your love and light.
Miss you like crazy!

Acknowledgments
To my loving husband Dwight, my copy editor Michelle Early, my sibs Michael & Robin, and all of my tribe: your love and support are unequaled. Thank you for rooting me to the finish line!

No matter what people say, being a third grader is not easy. In fact, being a third grader can come with lots of **CHALLENGES**. For example, Vic is challenged with how to be cool. His mother has caught him Googling "How to be cool in third grade." Being cool is not just important to Vic, but to many kids just like him. He finds there is a lot of **PRESSURE** to wear the newest styles of shoes and have really awesome school supplies like sports-themed notebooks and mechanical pencils.

Yet the more Vic's parents tell him to be himself, the more he tries to fit in with the crowd. Even though he may lack confidence when it comes to being cool, there are two things Vic is very **CONFIDENT** in: playing football and playing the cello. Yep, one of the unique things about Vic is that he plays the cello. His friend Anthony plays the cello as well, and his big sister Truth plays the violin. They occasionally practice together, encouraging one another to do their very best. And when they **COLLABORATE** it's quite a lyrical experience!

The Spring Concert at Maya Angelou Performing Arts School was just a few weeks away. Vic loved the **MELODIOUS** sounds he was able to make with his instrument, and his teacher Ms. Shieh was a great encourager.

"Vic," said Ms. Shieh, "I can tell you've been practicing! You are going to be our shining star in the spring concert!" Vic was beaming with joy! He wanted to jump up and down and do a happy dance! But wanting to keep up the appearance of being "cool," he gave a **MEAGER** smile and muttered "Thanks," while trying not to blush.

Finally, the day of the spring concert had arrived and everyone was talking about it excitedly at lunch. "Hey Anthony!" Vic exclaimed, "Did you remember to bring your bow tie? Is your family coming tonight? Did you practice your cello yesterday? What time did you go to bed last night? Did you get **SUFFICIENT** rest?" Vic had remembered his mom always saying he needed "sufficient rest."

8

Vic had just finished his stream of questioning when, much to his **DISMAY**, Billy slammed his lunch tray on the table across from the two boys, and sat down. Billy, whose real name was something fancy like "William Thelonious LeGrand," was trouble and everybody knew it. Vic thought Billy's parents should have named him "Bully" instead of "Billy" because that's exactly what he was. Not only was Billy the tallest fifth grader in the school, he was always rude to the third and fourth graders, and he was always **SARCASTIC**.

Billy had transferred to Maya Angelou Performing Arts School in 4th grade, and was really quite smart. His family had moved to Maryland from South Carolina and he was having a hard time adjusting. Billy had left all his good friends in South Carolina and was finding it hard to make new friends. He seemed proud of the fact that he was loud and **OBNOXIOUS**, although most kids avoided him for that very reason.

Billy's eyes locked in on Vic and Anthony and he decided which of the two boys he would target. The boys were secretly shaking in their shoes because Billy had a **REPUTATION** of being tough and he made the other kids feel small. "Playing the *cello* is for *babies*. Do we have any *baaaaaabies* at this table?" The kids fell silent as Billy glared into

Anthony's eyes. Anthony dropped his head and hoped to disappear. "Huh? Did you all hear me?" Billy said, raising his voice "DO WE HAVE ANY BAAAAAAABIES AT THIS TABLE?" As Billy's anger continued to rise, Zora ran as fast as she could to find a teacher!

Vic felt very uncomfortable and was nervous for his friend. Their classmate Ella was at the next table and could hear the **CONVERSATION** and felt badly for both boys. "I'm talking to YOU little baby!" Billy said, pointing directly at Anthony. Well Anthony had the same "being cool" issues as Vic and he also was afraid of Billy, so he dropped his head in fear.

"Somebody better hurry up and answer me!" Billy yelled, as he pounded his fist into his hand. Mr. Merc, the school principal, and Mr. Posey, the language arts teacher that Vic admired, had just led the school's Anti-Bullying **CAMPAIGN** and rally not long ago.

Vic tried to recall the things he had learned about facing a bully, but he was frozen in fear and couldn't remember what to do! So in an instant, he whispered a quick prayer in his mind, and within seconds he knew exactly what he had to do: STAND UP TO THIS BULLYING BILLY.

19

In a flash, Vic remembered witnessing Billy's **PRIOR** bullying, but he had been afraid to speak up—like when Billy took Justin's lunch last week, the day he shoved Rich up against the lockers and took his snack money, and the day he made Ella cry by teasing her about her new bright pink boots. Vic felt saddened that he had not helped his friends or even told a teacher about it. But remembering those things all of a sudden, Vic felt both angry and **EMPOWERED!**

20

Before he knew it, Vic gathered all the **COURAGE** he had. His mouth opened and he began to speak in a loud, firm voice. "Billy, leave Anthony alone!" Suddenly everyone turned their heads towards the

COMMOTION. There was murmuring throughout the cafeteria as the other children stared at the boys, wide-eyed and wondering what would happen next.

22

Caught off guard by Vic's courageous act, Billy slowly turned his **GAZE** toward Vic and all his **FURY** was now focused on him. If Billy had X-ray vision, he would have burned a hole right through Vic. Billy slowly backed his chair up from the table, and Vic did the same.

23

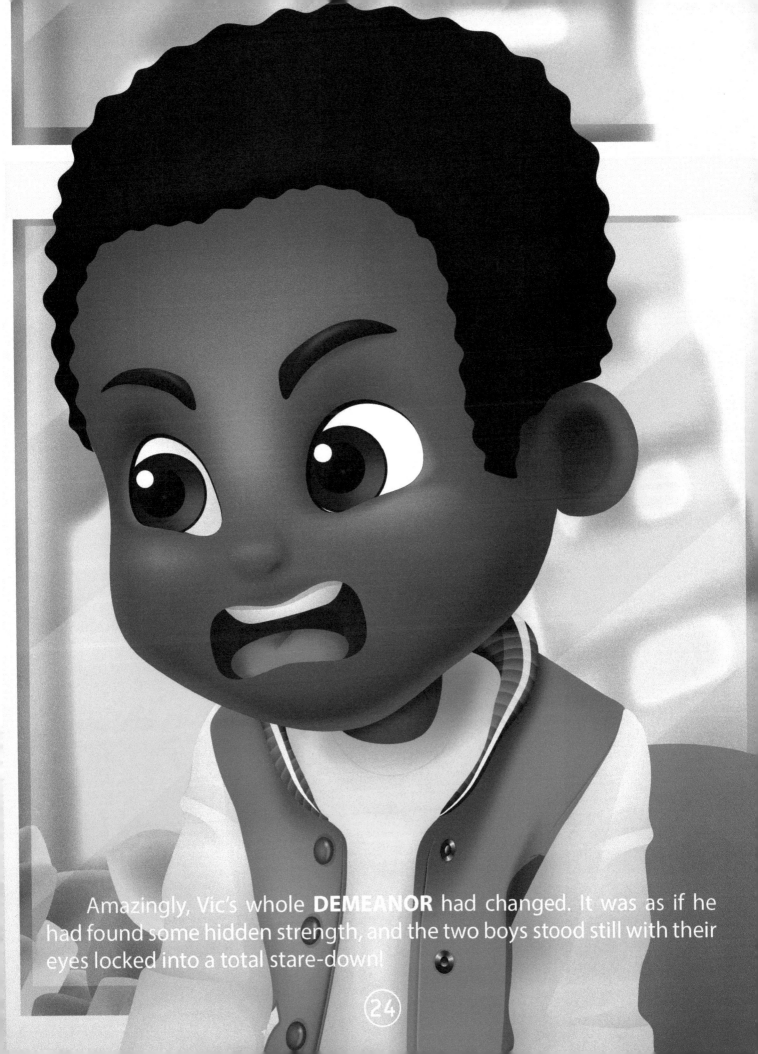

Amazingly, Vic's whole **DEMEANOR** had changed. It was as if he had found some hidden strength, and the two boys stood still with their eyes locked into a total stare-down!

In that moment, Mr. Posey approached the table with Zora by his side. Vic was relieved to see Mr. Posey because although he was tough on his students, he set high expectations and was fair, and the children grew to appreciate his leadership. He was always there to assist and **MEDIATE** when the children had differences.

Walking up to the table, Mr. Posey asked "Gentlemen, is there a problem?" "There sure is!" said Vic. "Billy is being a bully, and that's not cool!" "Yea!" exclaimed the rest of Vic's class, backing him up. Billy, who was surprised to see Vic's sign of **STRENGTH** along with the entire third grade in agreement, shrank down into his seat. "Gentlemen, please put your lunch trays away and come with me," said Mr. Posey. The boys got up and followed Mr. Posey down the hallway into Principal Merc's office.

last week

Billy's reputation was widely known, and Mr. Merc had disciplined him last week on his bad behavior. While the children never wanted to visit the principal's office for a disciplinary problem, they could be sure Mr. Merc would first try to help them understand why their behavior was not **APPROPRIATE**. The boys sat down at the table with Mr. Merc

HELP STOP BULLYING

27

Bullying is Bad

...e ...nds ...ot ...ullies

and Mr. Posey as Vic explained the events that led to them coming to the principal's office. He gave a full account of all the other events he had witnessed over the past few weeks that involved Billy being a bully. Billy, who was usually loud and **BOISTEROUS**, was surprisingly quiet. Vic thought he actually saw tears forming in Billy's eyes.

After hearing Vic's version of the events, Mr. Merc asked Billy for his account of what happened. Much to everyone's surprise, Billy sat quietly, feeling **REMORSEFUL**. Vic and the other children at school didn't realize that Billy simply did not know how to make new friends. Billy thought that by appearing to be rough and tough, he would become popular and fit in. He didn't realize that just being yourself is the best way to gain real friends.

Thankfully, Mr. Posey and Mr. Merc, aware of Billy's recent move to Maryland, seemed to sense what he was feeling. "Billy, we know that change and **TRANSITION** can be hard. But there are lots of really great kids here at Maya Angelou. We are a family, and we all want to help you

feel more comfortable in your new school," said Mr. Merc. With those words, Billy let out a small sigh of relief. He realized that being a bully was not who he was created to be. He just didn't know what to do and how to act around these new kids.

34

In that moment, Vic recalled the words from his Sunday school lesson: "Father **FORGIVE** them, for they do not know what they do." Filled with **COMPASSION**, Vic looked at Billy and said, "Hey, my birthday is coming up soon. Would you like to come to my party and get to know

some of the other kids in the school?" Inside, *this* time it was Billy who was jumping up and down! Like most kids, he *loved* birthday parties, but had not been invited to a single party since he had moved to Maryland.

"Why don't you **GENTLEMEN** stand and shake hands and try to be friends," said Mr. Merc, who had been observing all of this. The boys stood, shook hands, and smiled. For the first time, Billy felt like he could just be himself and that people might actually accept who he was. When the boys returned to the cafeteria smiling, all of the students stood and clapped and whistled!

Vic's mom had a tradition of asking him and Truth for their "Peak and Pit" for each day. The Peak was their highest point and the Pit was their lowest. This gave them an opportunity to share their experiences and talk through any challenges. At home that evening, Vic looked at his mom sincerely and said, "My pit was that you forgot to put pepperoni on my turkey sandwich." Mom quickly gave him a "side-eye" look. With

a slight grin Vic continued, "My peak was that I was strong and courageous, and I made a new friend!" As he shared everything that had happened with Billy, Mom **COMMENDED** Vic on a job well done and for practicing **FORGIVENESS**. The evening's musical concert was a huge success, and even Billy and his parents attended!

Bullying
is Bad

HELP!
I'M A BULLY

NO bullies Here

Make Friends not Bullies

Kicking

Intimidation

Name-Calling

Pinching

Exclusion

Embarrassment

Threats

Bullying

Assault

Bystander

DestroyingThings

Stealing

Teasing

Shoving

Cyberbullying

MeanNotes

Rumors

Hitting

Harassment

MeanLooks

I'm Against Bullying

The children learned some very important lessons that day: standing up to bullying is important, teachers are there to help, and bullies are people too. There is always a reason behind why people act the way they do. It may be because of fear, anger, or even shyness. Sometimes it's worth **EXPLORING** why they are behaving badly, so we can help them make a change for the better.

At bedtime, Vic lay awake reflecting on all he had experienced that day: leading with strength and courage, sharing his musical talents, and observing how his teacher and principal were good **ROLE MODELS.** He thought maybe he could be a role model too!

"I wonder what I will be when I grow up… other than really cool" Vic thought to himself as he smiled and drifted off to sleep…

Discovery Words

CHALLENGES – Interesting or difficult problems or tasks

PRESSURE – A strong influence or burden on the mind or emotions

CONFIDENT – Sure about one's own abilities

COLLABORATE – To work with someone else to achieve or do something

MELODIOUS – Having a pleasant musical tune

MEAGER – Lacking strength or number

SUFFICIENT – Enough; as much as needed

DISMAY – To cause (someone) to feel worried or disappointed

SARCASTIC – Using words that are opposite of what you want to say, especially when you want to be hurtful or seem funny

OBNOXIOUS – Very unpleasant or awful

REPUTATION – A widespread belief about someone or something

CONVERSATION – An exchange of ideas

CAMPAIGN – A series of planned actions carried out to reach a particular goal

EMPOWERED – Permitted or enabled; to give someone the power to do something

COURAGE – The ability to bravely face fear or danger

COMMOTION – A state of confusion; noisy

FURY – Wild anger or rage

DEMEANOR – How a person behaves or looks

MEDIATE – To bring people together to resolve a dispute or disagreement

APPROPRIATE – Right or proper for a specific purpose

STRENGTH – The state of being strong

BOISTEROUS – Noisy, loud or energetic

REMORSEFUL – Feeling regret or sorrow

TRANSITION – The process of changing from one condition or place to another

FORGIVE – To stop feeling angry towards someone
*Luke 23:34 (NKJV) "Father, forgive them, for they do not know what they do."

GENTLEMEN – Males who treat people in a courteous, polite way

COMMENDED – Praised or rewarded for doing a good job

EXPLORING – Trying to understand in more detail

ROLE MODELS – People whose actions set an example for others to follow

About the Author

Tish Thomas Cokely is a dream-chaser, mom, wife, Methodist pastor, inspirational blogger, sister-girl and life affirmer. She does her best writing while blasting various genres of music through her Bose headphones.

Aleko Wanted a Mohawk (2015) was her debut children's book, but she hasn't stopped there. Tish also has aspirations of writing screenplays and seeing her work on the big screen.

Currently an Equal Employment Opportunity Specialist with the federal government, she is a native of Dillon, South Carolina, and resides in Maryland with her husband and two of their three children.

Follow her inspirational blog at www.powerhousecommunications.blog and on Instagram and Twitter @1RevTish.

CPSIA information can be obtained
at www.ICGtesting.com
Printed in the USA
BVHW021631280819
557052BV00006B/67/P

9 781973 657828